Fantastic Folk Tales

THE FAST THAT NEVER HAPPENED

Indian Folk Tale

An imprint of Om Books International

Once upon a time, the monkeys living in a forest in India were very worried. They realised that they were getting fat due to overeating the whole day, every day. It was becoming difficult for them to swing from tree to tree! One day, a monkey fell down while hanging from a branch with a loud *Thud!*

The king of the monkeys soon came up with a solution, "We need to lose weight! I know how we can do that. We shall fast the whole day and will eat only in the evening. Do you all agree?" The monkeys did not like the plan at all, but none had the courage to disagree with the king.

Finally, the prime minister of the monkeys said, "Your Majesty, you have come up with a wonderful solution for our weight problem. But you see, by evening we will be very, very hungry. I suggest that we first go and collect all the food so that we don't waste any time in searching for it when the fast is over!"

The king agreed and two young monkeys were sent off to search for food. They came back with their arms overflowing with delicious, ripe bananas. But on seeing all the bananas, the monkeys became very hungry.

One of the monkeys bowed to the King and suggested, "Your Majesty, I think that we should distribute the bananas right away. That way we can start eating them the moment the fast is over, and we won't waste any time in distributing the bananas!"

The King agreed that it was indeed a very good idea and soon the bananas were distributed among all the monkeys.

By noon, the monkeys grew hungrier than before. One monkey suggested, "Your Majesty, if we peel our bananas right away, we will be able to save time when our fast ends!"

The king liked the idea and told the monkeys to keep their bananas peeled.

A little monkey looked at his banana eagerly and asked the king, "May I keep the banana in my mouth? I promise that I won't bite it or eat it till sunset!"

The King agreed and said, "Keep the banana in your mouth, but do not eat it!"

Once the food was in the mouth of the monkeys, they started salivating and desperately wanted to gobble the delicious, ripe bananas! They stared at each other, waiting for someone to give in to the temptation and bite into the banana.

Finally, one monkey said, "May we please take a bite and chew it? We will not swallow it, till the sun sets!" The King was craving to eat too, but didn't want to set a bad example for his subjects. Thus, he readily agreed to the suggestion.

Now, with the delicious, chewed banana in their mouths, all the monkeys quietly started swallowing the food.

The king suddenly noticed that his prime minister was swallowing the food. He looked around and realised that everyone was swallowing their food! He was angry and wanted to scold them. So, he swallowed his food and opened his mouth. Suddenly, there was a collective gasp and the king realised that he had broken his fast too!

The king felt very unhappy. To cheer up the king, the monkeys promised that they would keep the fast the next day. But the greedy monkeys were never ever able to fast for a day!